Heidi
Johanna Spyri

Young Readers' Classics

Abridgement by
Barbara Greenwood

Illustrations by
Richard Row

KEY PORTER BOOKS

Canadian Cataloguing in Publication Data

Spyri, Johanna, 1827–1901
Heidi

ISBN 1–55013–550–3

I. Greenwood, Barbara, 1940–   .   II. Row,
Richard   III. Title.

PZ7.S772He   j833'.8   C93–095560–9

Key Porter Books Limited
70 The Esplanade
Toronto, Ontario
Canada M5E 1R2

Typesetting: MacTrix DTP
Printed and bound in Hong Kong

94 95 96 97 98 6 5 4 3 2 1

1

From the little Swiss town of Mayenfeld a footpath leads up the mountains to the grassy pasturelands of the Alps. One sunny June morning, a young woman led a five-year-old child up the narrow path. By the time they reached the village of Dörfli, the child's cheeks were poppy red and she was dragging her feet. And no wonder! She had been bundled into every stitch of clothing she possessed — three dresses, one on top of the other, a red wool shawl around her shoulders, and hobnail boots over wool stockings.

"Hot!" the child said, plunking herself on the ground, as they paused at the gate of a small cottage.

"We're almost there," her companion encouraged her. "Another hour, that's all."

A voice called from the doorway, "Wait, Detie. I'm going up the mountain, too."

The two young women started off with the child trudging after them.

"Where are you taking her?" Barbel asked. "Isn't she your sister's child — Heidi, the orphan?"

"Yes. I'm taking her to live with her grandfather."

"What? Old Alp Uncle? How can you think of such a thing?"

"It's time for him to do his share," Detie said sharply. "Now that Mother's dead . . ." she hesitated, then said all in a rush, "I'm going to Frankfurt. I've been offered a good job and I mean to take it."

"But that old man lives up there like a hermit. Never goes to church. Talks to no one but his goats. And the rumors!" Barbel stopped and grasped Detie's arm. She dropped her voice and leaned close. "*You* must know, Detie, being family. What did he do all those years ago? Why are the villagers so afraid of him?"

Detie glanced around, looking for Heidi. Below them, the footpath twisted and turned all the way back to the village, but neither woman could see the child.

"There!" Barbel cried at last, pointing away from the path. "With Peter and his goats. He's late today. He should have been up in the pastureland long ago." She turned back to Detie. "No need to worry. He'll look after her."

"She can look after herself, that one. And just as well. Old Uncle has nothing now but that hut and some goats."

"But he used to have more?" Barbel was determined to know the story.

"Oh my, yes! He had the best farm around here at one time. But he wasted all his money gambling and had to sell it, or so my mother said. His parents died of the shame. And then he ran away to the city."

"Is that all?" The rumors Barbel had heard hinted at far worse.

"Isn't that bad enough? Years later he returned with a young son, Tobias. He wanted his kinfolk to take the boy in, but they shut their doors in his face. He was so furious that he took his boy and went to live up on the mountain. When Tobias was old enough, he left home to become a carpenter.

"We all liked Tobias. My mother was quite happy to have him marry my sister. But Adelheid was always delicate, you know. When Tobias was killed by a falling beam just after Heidi was born, the shock was too much for her. She died two months later. So Mother and I took Heidi to live with us. But now that Mother is dead and I have this job to go to . . ."

"Still, Detie, to leave the child with that old man." Barbel clucked in disapproval.

"Well, what am I to do?" Detie snapped. "I can't take her to Frankfurt with me."

Barbel shrugged. "Well, I'll leave you here. I have to

speak to Peter's grandmother. She spins for me in the winter. Good-bye, Detie. And good luck!"

Detie watched Barbel pick her way down a stony path to where a little cottage stood tucked into a sheltered hollow. The roof sagged and a shutter hung by one hinge. One strong gust from the mountain wind, Detie thought, and that old place will tumble right on top of Peter's mother and his blind old grandmother.

Detie put her hand up to shade her eyes and scanned the mountain slope. Where were they? Surely by now Peter must have taken the goats he herded for families in the village up to the high meadow. And Heidi? Angrily Detie started up the mountain. Heidi had better be with him, she thought.

The children had strayed far from the path as Peter led his goats from one tasty shrub to another. At first, Heidi had stumbled after him, panting in the heat. But the sight of the eleven-year-old boy leaping barefoot, over bush and stone with the goats was too much for her. She sat down and pulled off her boots and stockings. Soon the three dresses and the red shawl lay in a neat pile beside them. In nothing but her undershirt and petticoat, Heidi danced off to join Peter and the goats.

Peter grinned when he saw Heidi's new outfit but he said nothing. Heidi, on the other hand, chattered nonstop as she skipped beside her new friend. How many goats

did he have? Where was he taking them? Her stream of questions was interrupted by an angry shout. Detie had finally caught up with them.

"Look at you!" she scolded. "What have you done with your clothes? And those new boots I bought you? And the stockings I knitted?"

Heidi pointed down the mountain. Squinting, Detie could just make out the red of the shawl. "You bad girl!

Why did you take them off?"

"I was hot."

Detie turned to Peter. "Run down and fetch them," she ordered.

"I'm already late." Peter stood with his hands in his pockets, not moving.

Detie wanted to slap him. Instead, she smiled a tight little smile. "Come now, Peter," she coaxed. "You shall have this for your trouble."

At the sight of the shiny coin, Peter went leaping and dashing down the mountainside. He was back so quickly that Detie was smiling in earnest when she handed him the coin.

"You might as well carry the clothes," she said, "since you're coming up the mountain anyway."

Peter was happy to carry them. It was not often that he had a coin to tuck safely in his pocket.

Up the steep path they climbed, Heidi dancing beside the goats, feeling as free as air. She was the first to see the old man sitting outside his hut. He had built a wooden bench along the side of the cottage, and from there he could look right down the valley. Hands on knees, puffing on his pipe, he watched the little group approach.

Heidi ran straight up to him and held out her hand. "Hello, Grandfather."

"What's this?" he exclaimed. His voice was deep and

gruff. He drew his bushy eyebrows together in a fierce frown, and his long beard waggled as he clamped his teeth around the stem of his pipe.

"Good morning, Uncle." Detie came striding up the last of the path. "I have brought you Tobias's daughter."

The old man glared at Detie, then shouted at Peter, "Here, you! Be off with those goats. And don't forget mine."

As Peter swung his long stick to start the goats up the mountain again, Detie continued firmly, "She's come to stay with you, Uncle. I've done my share. Now it's your turn."

"Indeed!" snapped the old man. "And when she begins to fret for you, what shall I do then?"

"That is *your* business. I'm sure nobody's told me how to look after her these past five years. Just remember, you'll have to answer for it if she comes to any harm."

The old man rose suddenly. The look on his face made Detie step back quickly. "Be off with you!" he roared. "And don't show your face here again!"

"Very well then." Detie was backing away as she spoke. "Good-bye, Heidi. Good-bye, Uncle." She turned and hurried off without a backward glance.

Heidi didn't notice her aunt leaving. She was happily exploring the little meadow beyond the hut.

2

Heidi looked about her curiously. She peeped into the goats' shed, but it was empty. Beside the hut were three tall firs. She stood listening to the wind singing through their high branches. Then she went back to her grandfather, who was blowing great clouds of smoke from his pipe as he sat staring down the valley. She planted herself in front of him, hands behind her back.

"What do you want?" He continued to stare past her.

"I want to see what you have in the hut."

He looked at her, then rose. "Come along then. Bring your clothes."

"I don't need them anymore. I'm going to run about like the goats."

The old man turned to look at her. Her bright eyes were dancing with expectation. "So you shall," he said at last. "But bring them anyway. We'll put them in the cupboard."

Heidi picked up the bundle and followed him into the hut's one large room. In one corner stood a bed. A table had been pushed against the far wall. Most of another wall was taken up with a fireplace in which a kettle hung bubbling over the fire.

Grandfather walked across the room and opened a door in the wall. Heidi saw three shelves. One was neatly stacked with shirts, knitted stockings, and handkerchiefs. Another held plates and cutlery, a round loaf of bread, and a slab of cheese. The lowest shelf was empty. Heidi pushed her bundle right to the back of it. She wouldn't be needing those again!

"Where shall I sleep, Grandfather?"

"Wherever you wish, child."

Delighted, Heidi ran about the room inspecting every corner. Near her grandfather's bed stood a ladder. Heidi climbed it and found herself in a loft heaped high with sweet-smelling hay. From a tiny window she could look right down into the valley.

"I'll sleep here," she called down happily. "But I must have a sheet."

Grandfather went back to the cupboard. "This might do." He pulled out a heavy linen cloth.

In the loft he found that Heidi had piled and patted the

hay to form a small bed. Together they tucked the heavy sheet around it. The little girl sat back and regarded the bed thoughtfully. "Now it must have a coverlet," she announced.

"But I have none!"

"Then I'll just use more hay."

"Wait!" Grandfather climbed down and took a heavy linen sack from his own bed. "How is this?"

"Perfect! I can hardly wait to try it. How I wish it were bedtime now."

"We might have something to eat first," Grandfather suggested. And Heidi suddenly remembered that she had eaten nothing since early morning. "Oh, yes!" she said eagerly.

Back down in the big room, Grandfather pulled a small three-legged stool up to the fire and sat on it. He stuck a big piece of cheese on the end of a long iron fork and held it over the coals, turning it this way and that. For a while Heidi stood watching the cheese turn golden brown. Then she darted over to the cupboard. From the second shelf she took two plates, two knives and the loaf of bread.

"Very nice. You know how to be helpful," Grandfather said when he saw how Heidi had set the table. "There's something missing, though."

Heidi went back to look in the cupboard. Only one little bowl and a mug stood on the shelf. Heidi looked at the teapot steaming on the table, then picked up the bowl and the mug.

"Very good. You can think for yourself. But where will you sit?" Grandfather was sitting on the only chair. In a second Heidi had placed the stool by the table.

"Too short," Grandfather said. "But you wouldn't be

high enough in my chair either. We'll make you a table this way." He pushed the chair over to the stool. Turning back to the table, he poured milk into the little bowl and spread melted cheese on a round of bread. "Now eat," he said, placing them on the chair seat.

Heidi grasped the bowl in both hands and drank and drank. "I've never had such good milk in all my life," she said at last.

Smiling, Grandfather filled the bowl again. Heidi ate and drank and felt perfectly happy. Her grandfather perched on the corner of the table and began his own midday meal.

"Now we must do the chores," he said when they had finished. Out in the shed Heidi watched everything her grandfather did. First he swept the floor clean, then he spread fresh straw for the goats to sleep on that evening. Next he searched in the woodpile until he found four sturdy sticks. Working away with a knife and hammer, he soon had them fitted into holes he had made in a flat board.

"What do you think that is?" he asked when he had finished.

"A stool. A high stool so that I can sit at the table. How fast you made it!"

All afternoon Heidi followed her grandfather around as he swept and tidied and mended. Everything about her new home delighted her.

At dusk Heidi was sitting under the old firs, listening again to the wind sighing through their branches. Suddenly, a piercing whistle rang out. Down the mountain streamed the goats with Peter in their midst. As they ran past the hut, a white goat and a brown goat bounded gracefully out of the herd and up to Grandfather. He held out his hand and they began to lick it.

Heidi was so full of questions she didn't know where to start. "Are they ours, Grandfather? Do they live in the shed? What are their names? Why are they doing that?"

"I give them a little salt every evening to welcome them home. This is Schwänli and the brown one is Bärli. Now fetch me your little bowl and the bread."

When Heidi came dancing back, Grandfather milked the white goat. He filled Heidi's bowl with the frothy milk, then cut a slice from the loaf.

"Here's your supper," he said. "Eat it up and then go to bed. I have to look after the goats."

The old man and the goats disappeared into the shed.

"Good night, Grandfather," Heidi called when she had finished her bread and milk. Soon she was climbing the ladder to her bed where she slept as soundly as a princess in a palace.

3

Heidi was awakened the next morning by a shrill whistle and a flood of sunshine pouring in through the little round window. For a moment she didn't know where she was. Then she heard Grandfather's deep voice outside.

In a minute Heidi had jumped out of bed, pulled on her clothes, and darted down the ladder. Outside she found the goatherd, Peter, waiting with his flock. Schwänli and Bärli came tripping out of the shed in front of Grandfather.

"Would you like to go to the pasture, too?" he asked Heidi.

Heidi clapped her hands and jumped for joy.

"You must wash first." He pointed to a tub of water warming in the sun. "Come inside, General of the Goats," he said to Peter. "And bring your knapsack."

In the hut, the old man cut large chunks off the cheese and bread and dropped them into the surprised boy's sack. "Now the bowl." He tucked it in beside the bread. "Milk two bowlfuls for her at noon. And take care she doesn't fall into the ravine."

"Yes, Uncle." Peter could hardly take his eyes off Heidi's bread and cheese. He had barely half as much food for his own meal.

Heidi was so delighted to be going up the mountain that she danced and skipped ahead of Peter. The wind had blown away all the clouds and the sky was deep blue. Bright sunshine picked out the blue and yellow of gentian and primroses among the tufts of grass. Soon

Heidi had an armful of buttercups.

The pasture where Peter usually spent the day was at the foot of a rocky mountain peak. When they reached the highest point, Peter took off his knapsack and tucked it into a hollow where it would be safe from the strong mountain winds. Heidi wrapped her flowers in her apron and tucked it in beside the knapsack. Then she sat down beside Peter and gazed around.

The valley lay far below. Behind her a great field of snow stretched toward the heavens. Jagged rocks rose up on one side like towers and fell away on the other into a deep ravine. Everything was still except for a gentle breeze riffling through the bluebells and buttercups.

Peter, who had been up before dawn gathering his herd from the villagers, lay down and closed his eyes. But Heidi was too excited to sit still. She ran after the goats, making friends with each one. After a while, Peter woke up and began setting out their meal. He spread a square of cloth on the grass. On one side he put Heidi's large pieces of bread and cheese, on the other, his small ones. Then he called Schwänli and milked her.

"I love all the goats," Heidi said, watching him, "but Schwänli and Bärli are the prettiest."

"That's because Old Uncle brushes them and gives them salt and keeps their stalls clean. Now eat," Peter said, filling her bowl with milk.

"Is this milk for me?"

"Yes, and those big pieces of bread and cheese."

Heidi emptied the bowl and Peter filled it again. She broke a chunk off her bread, then held the rest toward Peter. "I've had enough."

Peter was speechless. He couldn't believe she was giving away so much food.

When he didn't take the bread, Heidi reached over

and put it on his knee. "Have the cheese, too," she said, laying it beside the bread.

Still looking puzzled, the goatherd bobbed his head as though to say thank you. Never in his life had he eaten such a large meal.

Peter was licking the last crumbs from his fingers when he suddenly turned his head and listened intently. Jumping up, he began to run.

"What is it, Peter? What is it?" Heidi ran after him.

A little goat was perched on the edge of the ravine. Reaching out to seize him, Peter tripped. As he fell, he managed to grab the goat's hind leg. The goat bleated in alarm, struggling to get free. If Peter let go, the goat would fall. If he didn't, they both might go over the edge.

"Heidi, help me!"

Heidi pulled a handful of sweet-smelling herbs and held them under the goat's nose. "Come, little goat. Be good," she coaxed. "You don't want to fall and break your bones, do you?"

The goat stopped thrashing and turned to nibble on the herbs. Peter seized the cord that held the goat's bell. Then, struggling to his knees, he hoisted the goat back onto safe ground.

"There!" Heidi grabbed the cord and led the goat away from the dangerous edge. When they were back down with the flock, Peter lifted his stick to beat the little animal.

"No, don't beat him!" Heidi cried. "Look how frightened he is."

"He deserves it," Peter snarled.

Heidi grabbed his arm. "I won't let you!"

Peter looked in astonishment at Heidi's snapping eyes. Then he dropped the stick. "He can go if you'll give me some of your cheese again tomorrow."

"You can have it all. Tomorrow and every day. But you must promise me not to hit the goats. Not this one or any one."

Peter shrugged. "It's all the same to me." He let the goat go and it went bounding back to the flock.

The day passed quickly. As the sun began to sink behind the great peak, Heidi called, "Peter, look, the mountain is on fire!"

"It's not fire. It's always like that in the evening."

"But what is it? Look, even that peak is glowing. Oh, what is the mountain called?"

"Mountains don't have names."

"Oh, look! The fire's gone out. Everything's gray." She turned sadly to Peter, who was peeling the bark off a new staff. "Why has it gone?"

"It does that every night." He stood and stretched. "Come on. Time to go home."

When they reached the hut, Heidi ran straight to Grandfather. "It was so beautiful," she cried. "The fire on

the mountain and the snow and the flowers. See what I've brought you!" She shook out her apron. But the flowers that tumbled to the ground were dry and crumpled like wisps of hay. "What's happened? They used to be so pretty."

"They like to be out in the sunlight," Grandfather said. "Not shut up in your apron."

"Then I shall never pick them again. Grandfather, why don't the mountains have names? And why does the fire come at night?"

"Jump into the washtub while I milk the goats," the old man said, "and then I'll tell you."

Over a supper of milk and bread, Heidi asked her questions again.

"The mountains do have names. The one you were on is called Falkniss. Did you like it up there?"

"Oh yes! Especially when the fire came. Why did that happen?"

Grandfather stroked his beard for a minute, then he said, "It's the sun's way of saying good night to the mountain. And it's a promise that it will be back again in the morning."

Heidi was delighted. She could hardly wait for the morning to see the sun again. That night she dreamt of goats leaping up the steep slopes of a shining mountain.

4

As the summer passed, Heidi grew strong and healthy. She loved playing in the high pasture. But one frosty morning Peter arrived blowing on his fingers to keep them warm, and Grandfather said, "Not today, Heidi. That strong wind might blow you right over the edge of the rocks."

The days grew dark and short, and Peter no longer came to fetch the goats. Now Heidi spent much of the time sitting on her stool near the fire watching Grandfather make goat's cheese or work with his hammer and nails at his carpenter's bench. His hands were always busy.

One day they were sitting working when the door flew open and Peter burst in. Snow clung to his hair, covered his jacket, and sat in clumps on his boots.

"You look like a snowman," Heidi laughed.

"Well, General, how are you?" Grandfather asked as Peter's suit of snow began to melt and drip. "I suppose, now that you have no goat army, you must chew on your pencil instead?"

Heidi was instantly curious. "Why must he do that?"

Peter, who was no great talker, just stood by the fire grinning, so Grandfather explained.

"Sometimes chewing a pencil helps with difficult things like reading and writing, isn't that right, General?"

Heidi was so interested in this new side of Peter that she peppered him with questions about school as he dried himself in front of the fire.

Finally Grandfather said, "All that talking is hungry work. Pull up a stool and we'll eat." He had made several more stools and so they had no difficulty settling around the table. As he was leaving that evening, Peter said, "I'm in school all week but I'll try to come again next Sunday. Grannie says come and visit her if you can."

This idea delighted Heidi. "We must go. Peter's grandmother expects us," she said several times over the next three days. But each time, Grandfather said, "The snow is too deep."

On the fourth day, the snow had frozen hard and crackled under foot. Heidi looked out the window forlornly. "Perhaps by now Peter's grandmother has grown tired of waiting for me."

Grandfather stared into the fire for a while. Then he sighed, stood up, and picked up a thick linen sack. "Put on your coat and scarf and come along," he said.

When Heidi ran outside wrapped in her warmest clothes, Grandfather was already seated on a large sled. He sat Heidi in front of him and wrapped her in the sack. Holding her tightly with one arm, he took hold of a large stick attached to a steering bar across the front of the sled, gave a mighty push with his feet, and they were off. Straight down the alp they flew, with a spray of snow from the runners streaming into their faces. They stopped, as if by magic, right at the door of Peter's hut.

Setting Heidi on her feet, Grandfather said, "You

must start up the mountain again well before dark." Then he turned the sled around and trudged away.

After she had watched her grandfather disappear up the mountain, Heidi opened the door of the hut and stepped in. By the glow from a small fireplace she could just see a little old woman bent over a spinning wheel.

"How do you do, Grannie?"

Peter's grandmother raised her head. She put out her hands, feeling in front of her until she touched Heidi. "Why — are you the child from up the mountain?"

"Yes, Grannie. I'm Heidi."

"The Alp Uncle's grandchild? Is that possible? How does the child look, Brigitta?"

A younger woman rose from the table where she had been sewing. She came over and took Heidi's face in her hands. "She is delicate like Adelheid but she has blond hair like Tobias. And she looks well."

"So Peter is right. The Old Uncle *is* taking good care of her. Who would have believed such a thing?"

As the women talked over her head, Heidi gazed around. She saw the shutters sagging on their hinges and said suddenly, "My grandfather will mend them for you. He can make anything. He made me a stool and a new tub for bathing. And he carved me a spoon and bowl."

"Do you hear what she says, Brigitta? Surely the child is mistaken."

"No, Grannie, he *will* mend the shutter," Heidi insisted. "Then the light can come in and you'll be able to see me."

"Ah, child, I can see nothing, nothing at all."

"But in summer, when the sun sets the mountains on fire, then you'll be able to see, won't you?"

"No, child. I shall never see the sun or the mountains again."

Heidi burst into tears. "Can't anyone make you see? There must be someone."

"Come here, my dear, and sit beside me." Grannie felt for Heidi's face and wiped away the tears. "When one is blind, it's good to hear a friendly voice. Tell me what you and the Alp Uncle do up on the mountain."

Heidi dried her tears. "Wait 'til I tell Grandfather. He's so clever. He'll make you see and he'll mend the hut, too. He can do anything."

Grannie didn't say a word. She just patted her young visitor's hand, and Heidi began to tell her about the two goats and how she had learned to brush and feed them.

Suddenly there was a great stamping of feet at the door and Peter burst into the room.

"What, home from school already?" Grannie cried. "How short the afternoon has been. How is the reading going?"

"Oh, the same." Peter shrugged and grinned at Heidi.

"Peter, Peter," the old woman sighed. "Remember,

you'll be twelve in February."

"Why does that matter?" Heidi asked.

"Look up on the shelf, child. Do you see an old book? It's full of beautiful prayers and hymns. I want so much to hear them again. But reading is too difficult for Peter." She sighed, and Peter's mother, who had been busy mending a jacket, said, "He'll learn one day. Fetch a lamp, Peter. It's getting dark."

"Oh," cried Heidi. "I must go!" She pulled on her coat and ran to kiss Grannie's cheek.

"But not alone," Grannie said. "Go with her, Peter. See her safely home."

The children had gone only a short distance up the mountain when they saw Grandfather striding toward them. "You've kept your promise, Heidi. Good!" He wrapped her in the linen sack and carried her back up the mountain.

At supper, Heidi said, "Tomorrow you must take your hammer and nails down to Peter's house and mend the shutters."

"Who says I must?" the old man demanded gruffly.

"I do! Grannie is afraid of the noise when the shutters bang. She thinks the roof will tumble down on their heads. Oh, and Grandfather, she can't see. She says no one can make her better, but you will, won't you? Can we go and help her tomorrow?"

Heidi had come to stand beside the old man as she spoke. He could look nowhere but into her eager, earnest face. "Tomorrow," he promised, after a long moment. "At least we can stop the banging."

The next afternoon Grandfather and Heidi once again swooped down the mountainside to Peter's hut. "Go in," the old man urged her. "And remember to start home before dark." Then he disappeared around the side of the cottage.

"Is it the child?" Grannie called the minute Heidi opened the door. "Oh praise be, he has let her come again!"

Heidi had no sooner pushed a low stool near the spinning wheel than a great pounding sounded on the other

side of the wall. Grannie was so startled that she almost knocked her spinning wheel over.

"Don't be afraid," Heidi said, setting the wheel firmly on its legs. "It's Grandfather. He's mending everything."

"Brigitta, run out and see! Could it really be the Alp Uncle?"

Brigitta found the old man nailing down a loose board. "Good day, Uncle," she said, nervously. "Mother and I are very grateful to you —"

"Enough!" he interrupted roughly. "I know well enough what you and the villagers think of me. Go back in the house. I can see for myself what needs doing."

Brigitta scurried in, glad to be away from the gruff old man, but Grannie listened to each hammer blow and marveled. "God has not forgotten us," she said.

And so the winter passed. Every day Grandfather wrapped Heidi in the coverlet for the ride down the mountain. Every day he stopped up more holes and nailed down more boards until the hut was snug and sound. Heidi was sad when she realized that not even Grandfather could make Grannie see again. But the old woman reassured her. "Your voice helps me to see," she said. "Tell me again about your days up on the mountains with the goats."

5

Two happy years passed. Then, in the early spring of the year that Heidi turned eight, two unexpected visitors arrived at the little hut on the alp. The first was the pastor from Dörfli. Heidi saw him climbing up the path one March morning when she was coming out of the goat shed.

"You must be Heidi." The old man sounded friendly. "Where is your grandfather?"

"By the fire, carving wooden spoons." Heidi opened the door and was surprised to hear the visitor say, as he stepped through the doorway, "Good morning, my friend."

Grandfather stood up but didn't shake the other man's hand. "Good morning, pastor." He pulled forward one of the new stools. "If you don't mind a hard seat, sit here."

"I've come to talk to you about something important . . ." The pastor stopped and glanced at Heidi.

"Take some salt to the goats, Heidi. And stay with them a while," Grandfather said. Sitting back down, he folded his arms and stared stonily at his guest.

"You must know why I'm here, neighbor," the pastor said quietly. "The child should be in school. She should have been there last year."

"The child thrives with the goats and the birds. She is well enough with them."

"But she must learn to read and write. Surely you see that?"

"And does the pastor suppose I would send a young child through storm and snow down the mountain?"

"True enough, neighbor. You cannot send her down the mountain. For her sake, then, do what you ought to have done long ago. Come back to live in Dörfli."

"Among people who despise me — as I despise them?"

"I promise you, friend, they do not feel that way. Make your peace with God and come back to live among your neighbors." The pastor stood and held out his hand. For a moment Grandfather ignored the offer of friendship. Then he grasped the pastor's hand in a firm grip, but his voice was equally firm.

"We will not come down to Dörfli and I will not send the child to school." He turned and opened the door.

"May God help you," the pastor said, shaking his head sadly as he went out the door and down the mountain.

Two days later, their second visitor arrived. Just as they were clearing the supper dishes from the table, Aunt Detie swept into the hut. She was wearing a hat with a curling feather, and her gown was so long that it dragged on the floor of the hut. Grandfather stared at her fine clothes in amazement.

"How well you look, Heidi," she exclaimed, all smiles despite the old man's silence. "I knew the air up here would be good for you. I've been thinking about you all this time and I've made some wonderful plans for you."

Heidi looked at her grandfather. What did Aunt Detie mean? The old man was clenching the stem of his pipe in his teeth as though he wanted to bite it in half. Still he said nothing and Detie chattered on.

"I know Heidi must be in your way, Uncle, so I've kept my ears open and now I've found a wonderful home for her with a very rich family in Frankfurt — the Sesemanns. The mother is dead and the daughter, Klara, is in a wheelchair. She needs a playmate, so her father wants someone to come and live with the family. Isn't that a wonderful opportunity? Heidi will be taught by the same teachers, learn how to live in a great house — who knows what might come of it? Why they might —"

"Have you finished?" grandfather interrupted.

"Well!" Detie snapped. "You needn't sound as if it's unimportant. This kind of opportunity . . ."

"You may tell them I'm not interested."

"I'll tell them no such thing. I've heard all about you down in Dörfli — how you won't send Heidi to school, how they had to send the pastor up here to speak to you. They'll take you to court if you refuse again. Did you know that? And if you think I'll let my only sister's child . . ."

"Silence!" Grandfather roared. "Take her, then, you with your ridiculous frills and feathers. And never set foot here again." He strode out of the hut.

"You've made Grandfather angry," Heidi said, her eyes flashing.

"Never mind that," Detie said briskly, throwing open the cupboard door. "Where are your clothes? We must be quick."

"I'm not going with you!"

"What did you say?" Detie whirled on her niece but seeing the stubborn look on Heidi's face, took a deep breath and smiled. "You heard what your grandfather said; he wants us to go. And believe me, my dear, you'll find it much more pleasant in Frankfurt. Here's your hat. Not very pretty but it will have to do. Come along, now."

"I'm not going."

"If you don't like it, you can always come back." Detie took Heidi by the arm and propelled her out the door.

"This evening? Can I come back this evening?"

"We'll be in Mayenfeld this evening," Detie said,

ignoring the question. "And tomorrow we'll be on the train. It moves so fast it's just like flying. It will bring you home again in no time."

As she spoke, Detie hurried down the mountain path, pulling Heidi after her.

"Peter's grandmother!" Heidi cried as they came to the hut. "I must say good-bye to her."

"No time. No time," Detie insisted as Heidi tugged at the hand holding hers. "We'll find a nice gift for Peter's grandmother in Frankfurt."

This idea pleased Heidi so much that she stopped struggling. "What could we get her?"

"Oh, something good," said her aunt. "Maybe some soft white rolls."

"Oh, yes!" Heidi agreed. "She has such trouble eating that hard black bread. Soft rolls would be wonderful. Let's hurry, Aunt Detie."

So it was that as they reached Dörfli, the villagers saw Heidi running ahead of her aunt.

"Poor child," they whispered. "She can hardly wait to get away from that terrible old man."

From that day on, the Alp Uncle looked more ferocious than ever when he stalked through Dörfli with his cheeses on his back to sell at the market. Only Peter's grandmother spoke up for him. But no one believed the blind old woman when she insisted he had been kind to Heidi.

6

"So this is the child." The tall woman looking down at Heidi did not appear to like what she saw. "That is a disgraceful hat she's wearing. Your name, child?"

"Heidi."

"What kind of a name is that?"

"If you please, Fräulein Rottenmeier," Detie bobbed a little curtsy to the housekeeper, "she was christened Adelheid, after her mother, my dead sister."

"She appears very small. Miss Klara requires a companion of her own age. How old is Adelheid?"

"Why I scarcely know. Ten, I believe," Detie stammered.

"Grandfather says I'm eight."

"What!" Fräulein Rottenmeier exclaimed. "Miss Klara is twelve. I don't think this will do at all. What have you learned, child? What books have you read?"

"None," replied Heidi.

"None? How did you learn to read, then?"

"I've never learned to read. Neither has Peter."

"You can't read at your age! Good gracious, Detie, what were you thinking of to bring me this child?"

But Detie was not about to give up easily. "If you remember, Fräulein Rottenmeier, you said you wanted an unspoiled child. This one fills the bill exactly. Now, if you will excuse me, my mistress is expecting me." Detie curtsied again and was out the door and down the stairs in a flash. Taken aback by Detie's sudden departure, Fräulein Rottenmeier hurried angrily after her, calling, "Wait just one moment, young woman."

Heidi stood where her aunt had left her. The room with its overstuffed chairs and long draperies seemed stifling to her. She longed to race after her aunt and beg to be taken back to the mountain, to her grandfather. She was about to turn and run when a soft voice said, "Come here."

Heidi looked around. In a wheeled chair by a small table sat a blue-eyed girl with long golden ringlets. She smiled at Heidi and held her hand out. "Shall I call you Heidi or Adelheid?"

"My name is Heidi. That's what everyone calls me."

"Then I shall call you that, too. And can you really not read?"

Heidi shook her head and the girl laughed and clapped her hands. "What fun lessons will be! We will teach you to read instead of doing boring old history."

Heidi shook her head. "I'm going home tomorrow, as soon as I get some white rolls for Grannie."

"But you came to keep me company. I'm sure you'll like it here. And my tutor is very kind. You'll learn to read in no time."

Fräulein Rottenmeier came bustling back into the room. "That tiresome girl was out the door before I could get downstairs. We'll just have to make the best of it for now." She clapped her hands sharply and called, "Tinette? Sebastian?" Double doors at the back of the room swung open.

"Tinette, make a room ready for the young miss." A

sharp-faced girl in a maid's apron and frilly cap threw a disdainful glance at Heidi, then flounced off.

"Sebastian, we will have dinner now. Take Miss Klara in."

Heidi could not take her eyes off Sebastian. It was not his smart jacket with big round buttons that attracted her, but his face. "You look just like Peter," she said, as Sebastian pushed Klara in her chair through the double doors.

Fräulein Rottenmeier threw up her hands in horror. "You must not speak to servants in that familiar way! I see I shall have to teach you everything."

Klara smiled reassuringly, but Heidi paid no attention. On a plate beside her place at the table sat a beautiful white roll. Only Sebastian saw her slip it into her apron pocket. He smiled to himself, knowing that if he laughed out loud, the stern housekeeper would fire him.

All through dinner Fräulein Rottenmeier lectured Heidi on how she was to behave in a gentleman's house. Heidi barely heard a word. She was so tired from her long day that she was fast asleep at the table when Sebastian came to take away the dessert plates. She didn't wake even when he carried her upstairs to the little corner room that Tinette had made ready for her.

When Heidi awoke in the morning, she couldn't remember where she was. Everything looked strange — the large room, the high white bed, the washstand in the corner, the two armchairs. Light shone through long, white curtains, but the air was stuffy. In a panic, Heidi jumped out of bed and ran to the window. It was so high up that she had to stand on tiptoe to see over the sill. Even then, all she could see was a bare brick wall. Surely if she managed to open the window and look down, she would see grass and trees and breathe fresh air! But no matter how hard she tried, the window would not budge.

Feeling like a caged bird, Heidi slowly dressed. She was sitting on a low stool wondering what to do next when Tinette popped her head in at the door. "Breakfast," she said. "Downstairs." Although her scornful tone was not at all inviting, Heidi followed her down to the dining room where Klara had been waiting for some time.

Heidi sat quietly all through breakfast, but as soon as the two girls were alone in the library, Heidi asked, "How do you look out, Klara? How do you see the ground from the house?"

"Why we open a window, of course!"

"But they won't open. I've tried."

"You must ask Sebastian. Now tell me about your life up on the mountain."

Heidi was so relieved to hear that Sebastian would open the window for her that she chatted happily about Grandfather and the goats and the wonderful evening sun that lit up the mountain like fire.

Out in the hall Fräulein Rottenmeier was waiting for the schoolmaster. "A word, Herr Usher," she said, beckoning him into the dining room. "We have a young visitor, a companion for Miss Klara. Herr Sesemann has left orders that she is to be treated as one of the family. But I fear she is not suitable. I was appalled to discover that the girl does not even know her alphabet."

"But, Fräulein, I do not mind teaching the child her alphabet."

Fräulein Rottenmeier's lips tightened angrily. "If the child holds Miss Klara back in any way, I consider it to be your duty to inform Herr Sesemann immediately."

The tutor bowed politely. He had just turned to leave when they were both startled by a crashing sound. Fräulein Rottenmeier swept past him and flung open the library door. A small table lay on its side. Books and papers were strewn everywhere. Heidi was running toward the other door.

"That wretched child! What has she done now?" Fräulein Rottenmeier cried.

"It was an accident." Klara was laughing so hard she could barely speak. "She heard the carriages in the street and ran to look at them."

"You see what I mean, Herr Usher? The child has no idea how to behave in polite society. Where has she gone?"

She hurried downstairs and found Heidi standing in the open doorway looking puzzled.

"I thought I heard the wind in the fir trees. But I can't see them anywhere," Heidi said sadly.

"Firs? Do you think we live in a forest? Come upstairs immediately and let us have no more of this wild running about. You will sit quietly and pay attention when you are in the library. Do you understand?"

Heidi sighed. "Yes, Fräulein Rottenmeier."

By the time Sebastian and Tinette had cleaned up the mess in the library, there was no time left for lessons. Because of her illness, Klara always rested in the afternoons. Fräulein Rottenmeier liked to spend this time in her own room, so she said to Heidi, "You may do as you like while Miss Klara is resting, but stay out of mischief."

Heidi knew exactly what she wanted to do, but she needed help. She sat on the top step of the stairs until Sebastian appeared carrying a tray.

"Excuse me," she began politely.

As they walked, Heidi noticed a box that her guide had slung over his back. "What's that on your back?" she asked.

"A music box. I turn the handle to play the music and people give me pennies."

Before Heidi could ask more questions about this intriguing job, they had reached the church. Its large wooden door was closed.

"How do I get in?"

"Don't know."

"Perhaps I could ring that bell." She pulled on the cord with all her might. From a long way away came a faint clanging.

"You must wait here while I go up," Heidi said, "and then show me the way back."

"What will you give me?"

"What do you want?"

"Another four pennies."

Just then the door creaked open. An old man peered out. "Be off with you," he barked at them.

"But I want to go up the tower," Heidi said.

"Go home," the caretaker snapped. "And don't ring my bell again or I'll call the constable."

"Please," Heidi pleaded. "Just once."

"Oh, very well," he grumbled. "Come along then."

Taking Heidi's hand, he led her inside. "You stay there," he said to the boy and slammed the door.

They climbed and climbed. The dark staircase grew narrower and the steps tinier until finally they saw light above them. They came out onto a platform surrounded by high walls. In each wall was a large window. The old man lifted Heidi so that she could look out, but all she saw was a sea of roofs and towers and chimneys.

"Oh," she exclaimed, disappointed. "It's not at all what I hoped for."

"What would a child like you know about views?" sniffed her companion. "Well, you've had your look. Come along down. And mind you leave my doorbell alone after this."

Halfway down, the staircase widened out to a landing where the caretaker had his room. Beside his door was a basket in which lay a large gray cat. She growled warningly when Heidi came near, but the old man said, "She won't hurt you while I'm here. Come and see her kittens."

"Oh, how lovely!" Heidi cried when she saw seven tiny kittens nestled beside their mother.

"Would you like one?"

"Oh, yes!" Heidi almost danced with delight.

"Have as many as you like," said the caretaker, seeing an easy way to rid himself of extra mouths to feed.

"But how can I carry them?"

"I'll bring them to you. Tell me where you live."

"At Herr Sesemann's house. It has a golden dog's head on the door with a ring in its mouth."

The old man had lived in the neighborhood for many years and knew the house well.

"Who shall I ask for? *You* don't belong to Herr Sesemann, do you?"

"No, but Klara will be delighted to have the kittens. Oh, let me take these two with me. The white one for Klara," she said, popping the little wriggling creature into one apron pocket, "and the orange one for me."

When she opened the church door, the boy was sitting on the steps, waiting for her.

"Which way to Herr Sesemann's?" Heidi asked.

"Don't know."

"The roof goes like this," Heidi said, making a steeple with her hands, "and one of the windows looks out on a big gray house."

That was all the boy needed. In no time they were

standing in front of the door with the dog's head knocker. Suddenly it flew open.

"Quick! Quick!" Sebastian urged, pulling Heidi into the house and slamming the door in the boy's face. "You're late. Into the dining room with you. They're already at table."

When Heidi walked into the dining room, Fräulein Rottenmeier stared at her stonily. Even Klara sat quietly, her eyes fixed on the plate in front of her. With a pounding heart, Heidi slipped into her chair.

"You may serve the soup, Sebastian. As for you, Adelheid, I will speak to you later about your disgraceful conduct. To leave the house without telling anyone —"

"Meow."

"What did you say? How dare you mock me!"

"But I didn't —" Heidi began when she was interrupted.

"Meow, meow."

"Heidi," Klara gasped. "Why do you keep doing that? You can see how angry —"

Almost in tears, Heidi burst out, "It's the kittens!"

"Kittens! Sebastian, get rid of them at once. At once!" And the housekeeper rushed out of the room.

Sebastian was laughing so hard he had to set down his tray. Even Klara had to clap her hand over her mouth.

"Poor Fräulein Rottenmeier is afraid of cats," she said, when she was able to speak. "Let me see them. Oh, how sweet," she cried, as Heidi held out the white one. Klara cradled it in her hands. "Sebastian, can you find a place

for them? Somewhere safe so we can play with them when we're alone?"

"I'll take care of them, Miss Klara. A nice little basket where the Fräulein won't find them."

On the following morning, Sebastian had no sooner shown the tutor into the library, than the doorbell rang again. On the steps stood a ragged boy.

"What do you mean by ringing this bell? Be off with you!"

"I want to see Klara."

"A dirty brat like you? How do you know Miss Klara?"

"I showed her the way home yesterday. She has long blond braids."

A mischievous smile lit Sebastian's face. "Well, well," he said. "Come in. You may play your music box for Miss Klara. She'll like that. Follow me."

Sebastian knocked on the library door, then opened it. "A boy to see Miss Klara," he announced.

"May he come in, Herr Usher?" Klara asked, but the boy was already in the room playing his music box.

Klara and Heidi were enchanted. They clapped their hands and asked him to play again. Herr Usher kept clearing his throat as though he were about to say something. Suddenly Fräulein Rottenmeier rushed into the room.

"What is going on here? Who is this? Sebastian, take him away at once!"

The butler quickly bundled the boy out of the library and down the stairs.

"Here you are," he said at the front door. "Eight pennies for seeing the young miss home and eight more for the music."

The morning's surprises were not over. No sooner had Herr Usher settled his students back to work, than the doorbell rang again. A large covered basket for Miss Klara!

"For me? Let me see."

"Perhaps it would be better to wait until after the lesson," Herr Usher suggested.

But it was too late. As soon as Sebastian set the basket down, the cover popped open and one, two, three kittens jumped out and began to scamper around the room. Heidi scooped up two and ran after the third, as more kittens escaped from under the wicker lid.

"There!" Klara cried, pointing under the table. "And there!"

"Young ladies, young ladies!" the tutor protested, but neither girl paid any attention to him. They were too interested in the kittens. With Sebastian's help, the kittens had all been returned to the basket when Fräulein Rottenmeier appeared.

"What is happening here? Adelheid, get up off the floor." Fräulein Rottenmeier was so busy scolding Heidi that she didn't notice Sebastian whisk the basket out of the room.

"What is to be done with you, Adelheid? You have no sense of how to behave. None at all. I know of only one punishment that will have any effect on a child such as you. You will spend the rest of the day in the cellar with the rats."

Heidi had no idea what a cellar was, but Herr Usher looked shocked and Klara gasped, "No, Fräulein Rottenmeier! You must wait until Papa comes home. *He* will decide."

Fräulein Rottenmeier frowned and swept out of the room. After Sebastian returned, he told the girls that he had hidden all the kittens in the attic. When Fräulein Rottenmeier was out of the house, he promised to spirit them into Klara's room for the girls to play with.

In the evenings, Heidi told Klara stories about her life in the mountains, and during the day she tried to learn how to read. But no matter how patient and gentle Herr Usher was, she did not seem to be able to sort out one letter from another. As the days passed, only the slowly growing pile of white rolls, hidden in a shawl at the bottom of her closet, comforted her. At least, when she went home, she would have a wonderful present to give to Peter's grandmother.

8

"Listen to this," Klara said one day when they were sitting having breakfast. Sebastian had handed her a fat envelope from Paris, which had arrived by mail that morning. "Papa is coming home at last. He says he will arrive the day after tomorrow."

"Well, that *is* good news," Fräulein Rottenmeier said. "And it reminds me — Klara, we must go through your wardrobe. Several of your dresses are too small and would do quite well for Adelheid. We must have her dressed more respectably by the time your papa returns."

Heidi thought nothing of this until later that day as she sat with Klara in the library. The older girl was reading aloud from a book of fairy tales when Fräulein Rottenmeier stormed in.

"Just look at what Tinette found at the bottom of

Adelheid's closet. I couldn't believe my eyes! All tied up in a dirty shawl." She shook the shawl and little white rolls as hard as pebbles rolled out and bounced on the carpet. "The idea of keeping food in a clothes closet. Throw this stale bread out, Tinette, and this disgusting shawl and hat with it."

"No! No!" Heidi went pale. "I must keep the hat for going home! And the rolls are for Peter's grandmother!" She tried to run after Tinette, but Fräulein Rottenmeier caught her firmly by the shoulders and pushed her back into the library.

Heidi crumpled to the floor by Klara's chair. "They were for Grannie," she sobbed. "She can't eat the black bread. What am I to do? What am I to do?"

"Heidi, please don't cry," Klara begged. "You shall have as many rolls as you wish. I promise."

"As many as I had saved up?"

"Even more! And they'll be soft, fresh ones. Those had gone hard. They wouldn't have been any good."

Although Klara's promise comforted Heidi, she still had red eyes when she appeared at the supper table. The sight of a fresh roll brought more tears to her eyes. As she blinked them back, she saw Sebastian winking at her and pointing to his head. What could he possibly mean?

The mystery was solved later that evening when she went upstairs. There, on her bed, was the battered old

straw hat. Sebastian had saved it from Tinette and the garbage. Tenderly, Heidi smoothed out its bent brim and tucked it away in the back of her closet.

Two days later, Heidi and Klara were sitting in Klara's room looking at pictures in a book when they heard carriage wheels clattering on the cobblestones outside. A few minutes later, Herr Sesemann walked into the room.

"Papa!" Klara cried, holding out her arms. Heidi walked to the far side of the room and waited quietly while father and daughter kissed. Then Herr Sesemann turned and held out his hand to her.

"And this is our little Swiss girl. Are you happy here, my dear? Are you and Klara good friends?"

"Klara is always good to me," Heidi replied.

"Heidi makes me happy, Papa," Klara said quickly.

"I'm glad to hear it. Now I must have some luncheon. I'll be back to talk after I've eaten."

In the dining room Fräulein Rottenmeier was waiting with a sour look on her face.

"I am sorry to report, Herr Sesemann, that our little visitor has not worked out well. Klara has been upset and disturbed by her. We were looking for someone with a sweet, unspoiled nature, but this one does nothing but disrupt the household with animals and ragged urchins and —"

"Good heavens, Fräulein, what a list of calamities! And here I thought Klara seemed much better. Ah, well, I'll ask her about all this later."

When Herr Sesemann entered the library, Heidi jumped to her feet politely.

"My child, would you fetch me — now what was it I wanted? a glass of cold water?" Herr Sesemann smiled and held the door open.

Heidi darted from the room and Herr Sesemann sat down beside his daughter's bed. "Now, my dear, tell me truthfully, what has been happening? What is this about your little playmate bringing animals into the house?"

When Klara had explained to her father about the kittens and the boy with the music box and the white rolls, he burst out laughing.

"So you are quite content with your little companion? You don't want me to send her away?"

"Oh no, Papa! We have had such fun. Every day is a surprise. I feel so much better when I have Heidi to talk to."

"Ah, here she is." Herr Sesemann held out his hand for the glass of water that Heidi was carrying carefully. "Thank you, my child. Now I have a surprise for you both. I must go back to Paris next week, but Grandmamma will be coming for a nice long visit."

A week later, when a carriage stopped at the front door, Heidi was sent up to her room.

"Frau Sesemann will want to see Klara first," Fräulein Rottenmeier explained. But before long Tinette rapped at the door, summoning Heidi down to the library.

Klara's grandmother was sitting in a low chair with her feet on a little stool. Heidi curtsied as Fräulein Rottenmeier had taught her, then took the hand that was held out to her. It was soft and white. Everything about this lady seemed soft and white, from her hair, which looked like a cloud, to her lace cap with the white ribbons that fluttered behind. Heidi loved her the moment she set eyes on her.

"And what is your name, child?"

"My real name is Heidi, Madam, but if I must be called Adelheid, I'll try to remember."

Frau Sesemann cast a surprised look at the housekeeper, who stood in the doorway.

"I am sure you will agree, Madam, that the child should be called by her proper name."

"My good Rottenmeier, there is nothing wrong with the name Heidi. Now, please fetch the parcel on my bed. I have brought some books for Heidi."

Fräulein Rottenmeier sniffed. "Books will do her no good. She hasn't learned to read. If Herr Usher didn't have the patience of a saint, he would have given up on her ages ago."

As the housekeeper left the room, Frau Sesemann asked, "Is this true, Heidi? Can't you read?"

Heidi sighed. "No, Madam. Peter says reading is too difficult, so I knew I wouldn't be able to."

"This Peter sounds like a very strange person. And you must call me Grandmamma."

"Oh, thank you. I have been calling you that but Fräulein Rottenmeier said —"

"Never mind about Fräulein Rottenmeier. And never mind about Peter either. We will soon have you reading.

And here's a little promise for you: As soon as you can read all the way through one of my books, you shall have it for your very own."

From that day on, while Klara was resting, Heidi spent every afternoon in the library with Grandmamma looking through the beautiful story books. One day she found a picture of a green meadow. Two frisky goats played around a boy who stood leaning on his stick. Suddenly tears poured down her cheeks.

"What is it, child? What has upset you?"

But Heidi could not tell Grandmamma how she longed for the mountains and Grandfather. Fräulein Rottenmeier had warned her that Klara and Herr Sesemann would think her ungrateful if she complained and asked to go home. She couldn't bear to hurt kind Grandmamma so she just shook her head and wiped the back of her hand across her eyes.

"My dear, I've noticed that you seem unhappy sometimes. If you cannot tell anyone what your trouble is, it is a good idea to ask God for help. Have you learned to pray?"

"I used to with my first grandmother. But I've forgotten how."

"You must start again. The good Lord will help you."

"I'll pray tonight," Heidi promised. She would ask God to send her home.

9

Grandmamma's visit was almost over when Herr Usher came to her one day. "The most unusual occurrence," he began. "I had almost given up hope —"

"Are you trying to tell me," Grandmamma interrupted gently, "that Heidi has learned to read?"

The young man stared in surprise. "Yes, indeed — so unexpected, so . . ."

Frau Sesemann just smiled, and that day at the dinner table Heidi found her favorite story book at her place.

"Is it for me?" she asked. "To keep forever?"

"Forever," Grandmamma said.

"Even when I go home?"

"But you won't go home for a long time, will you, Heidi?" Klara said. "I would miss you so much."

Klara felt so sad when Grandmamma left that Heidi

couldn't bear to mention how much she would like to go home. She had confided to Grandmamma that God had not answered her prayers, and Grandmamma had said she must have patience.

"He is so much wiser than we are, my dear. Perhaps He has a reason for asking you to wait."

So Heidi tried to be patient, but no matter how much she enjoyed the hours she spent with Klara, she could not help longing for the sound of the wind through the fir trees and the taste of milk fresh from Schwänli. As the days passed, she ate less and less. She grew pale and thin and quiet.

Winter turned into spring. Klara was allowed to take short carriage rides in the fresh air. But even on these outings, Heidi saw only brick walls and stone streets. If birds sang in Frankfurt, the sound of the carriage wheels muffled their song. Heidi grew more homesick as each week went by.

Fräulein Rottenmeier was also having problems. She had developed a nervous habit of suddenly looking over her shoulder, for something strange was going on in the Sesemann house. No matter how carefully the house-keeper checked the locks on the doors and windows each evening, in the morning the big front door stood wide open. The first time it happened, Sebastian and Tinette were sent running to check every room. Nothing was missing and no one was found hiding in the house. But morning after morning, the door was open.

After a month of this, Fräulein Rottenmeier persuaded Sebastian and John the coachman to sit up and watch the front door. The two settled into a room off the front hall. As the hours passed and nothing happened, their eyelids drooped and soon they were asleep. Sometime in the night a cold draft wakened Sebastian. He jumped up and ran out into the hall. The door stood wide open. He turned to call John and an icy shiver ran up his spine. On the stairway, just drifting around the corner, was a figure in white. Shaking like leaves in a wind, the two men locked themselves into the room off the hallway and waited for dawn.

When Fräulein Rottenmeier heard about the figure in white, she wrote immediately to Herr Sesemann. Although she had been careful to keep the mysterious happenings from Klara and Heidi, she pointed out to him that the thought of ghosts in the house might seriously affect the health of his delicate daughter. Her letter brought Herr Sesemann at once.

"This is nonsense," he said, the minute he set foot in the house. "Ghost, indeed! Sebastian, how could a grown man be so foolish? I will sit up tonight and we will get to the bottom of this."

That evening, when the household was in bed, Herr

Sesemann settled down with several candles and a book to wait for the ghost. His pocket watch was showing one o'clock when a slight sound caught his attention. Was that soft click a key turning in a lock? Cautiously he edged out into the hall. The front door stood open. Moonlight flooded in. Silhouetted on the doorstep was a small figure in white.

"Who's there?" shouted Herr Sesemann, holding up the candle to light the hallway.

The little figure cried out and turned. In the candle-light stood Heidi, barefooted, in her long, white night-gown.

"My dear child . . ." Herr Sesemann put down the candle and took Heidi's icy hands in his warm ones. "What does this mean? Where were you going?"

Heidi blinked at the light. "I don't know."

"Come and sit down and tell me what the trouble is."

Herr Sesemann led Heidi into the small room beside the hall. Embers still burned in the grate, warming the room, but even after Herr Sesemann had wrapped a shawl around her, Heidi's teeth still chattered.

"Don't be afraid," he said soothingly. "Tell me where you were going."

"I was looking for the trees," Heidi began. "Every night when I close my eyes, I see the firs outside my window at Grandfather's. The wind sings through the

branches and I run outside to see the stars shining in the heavens. It is so beautiful. But when I open my eyes, it's all gone. All I see are walls and streets. And I feel a great stone sitting on me, right here." Heidi put her hand over her heart.

Herr Sesemann sighed and took hold of the cold little hands again. "Come, I'll tuck you into bed. And I promise you, tomorrow we'll do something about this problem of yours."

At seven the next morning, Herr Sesemann rapped loudly on the housekeeper's door. "Make haste, Fräulein," he called. "There is a journey to prepare for."

Then he went to his daughter's room.

"I know how much you love Heidi, Klara. But she is so homesick that she walks in her sleep. I was shocked to see how pale and thin she is. We must think of her and not just ourselves, my dear."

Klara wiped a tear from her eye. "You're right, Papa. I mustn't be selfish. Please ask Sebastian to bring Heidi's trunk to my room. I want to pack some surprises for her. Oh, and Papa, there's something else." Klara told her father the whole story about the little white rolls, and he went off to tell Fräulein Rottenmeier to have a basket of fresh rolls packed immediately.

Heidi had no idea why Tinette had arrived in her room with orders to dress her in the best of Klara's out-grown dresses. She was even more puzzled when she arrived in the dining room to find a tearful Klara holding out her arms and crying, "How I shall miss you!"

Herr Sesemann smiled. "Sit down, my child. Has no one told you? You're to go home today. Right after breakfast."

"Home?" Heidi turned white. She could scarcely breathe, her heart was pounding so hard. "Home to Grandfather?"

"You *do* want to go?"

"Oh, yes, please!"

"Well, then, so you shall. Eat a hearty breakfast and then go off with Klara while we get everything ready."

Heidi was too excited to eat and Klara was already finished, so Sebastian wheeled Klara in her chair back to her bedroom. In the middle of the floor stood a half-full trunk.

"Come and see what I've packed for you," Klara said. The trunk held stacks of dresses and aprons, handkerchiefs and sewing things. The greatest treasure of all, though, was a deep basket piled with soft white rolls. The girls looked delightedly through the trunk, forgetting their coming separation until Herr Sesemann called, "The carriage is ready."

Then Heidi suddenly realized how much she loved Klara. She flew into her friend's outstretched arms.

"I shall miss you so much," Klara said. "But Papa has promised that if I get stronger, we will come to visit you in the mountains."

"Oh, Klara, you must come! The mountains will make you stronger, just the way they made me stronger."

Herr Sesemann called again.

"My book!" Heidi cried and ran upstairs. Although Grandmamma's story book was Heidi's greatest treasure, she also needed the old straw hat she had hidden at the back of her closet. Without it, she was afraid Grandfather would not recognize her in Klara's fine dress and cape.

In the hallway everyone had gathered to say good-bye to her. Heidi laid the little hat on top of the basket full of rolls.

"Adelheid, you cannot leave this house carrying that shabby thing," said Fräulein Rottenmeier, twitching the hat off the sparkling white cloth that covered the basket.

Heidi cast a stricken look at Herr Sesemann.

"Let the child take what she wishes," Herr Sesemann said sharply. "Now, my dear, here is a letter and a package for your grandfather. Take good care of them. Sebastian will see you safely home."

Clutching the precious hat under one arm and the letter and package under the other, Heidi was lifted into the carriage.

"Good-bye. I'll write to you," Klara called, waving.

"A safe journey," Herr Sesemann said. "And don't forget your friends in Frankfurt."

"Thank you for everything," Heidi called out the window as John the coachman flicked his whip. And they were off to the railroad station.

10

Two days later, the weary travellers arrived in Mayenfeld. As the train puffed back down the valley, Sebastian set down Heidi's trunk and basket on the platform, then looked around in dismay. Mountains rose on all sides. There were no paved roads and no carriages. How did one travel in this backward place? At that moment a cart rumbled to a stop beside the little station. Sebastian strode over to the carter to ask for help.

"If the trunk's not too heavy, I can take it up to Dörfli," the man offered, "and the child as well."

"It's all right, Sebastian," Heidi assured him. "I know the way from Dörfli."

Sebastian felt a little guilty as he watched the cart roll away, but he hadn't really wanted to climb a mountain. With a sigh of relief, he sat down to wait for the next train.

The carter, a Dörfli man, was curious about the child and her luggage. "You must be the girl who used to live with the Alp Uncle," he said. "Didn't they treat you well, down there in the city?"

"They were very kind," Heidi said.

"Then why didn't you stay?"

"Because I'd much rather be up on the mountain with Grandfather."

The carter raised an eyebrow at that. When they reached Dörfli, Heidi grabbed her basket and started up the path. "Grandfather will come for the trunk," she called back. So the carter was left to pass on to the curious villagers the amazing news that Heidi had chosen to come back.

Heidi hurried as fast as she could to Peter's hut.

"Grannie, Grannie!" she cried, as she reached the door.

"That's just how Heidi used to sound," said the old woman, but before she could say another word, Heidi was in her arms.

Grannie patted Heidi's face. "Dear child, you're back! Oh, God is good!"

"And I'll never leave again," Heidi promised. "Here's a present for you." She pressed one of the rolls into Grannie's hands. "Now you won't have to eat that hard, black bread."

Just then Brigitta appeared in the doorway. "Heidi!"

she gasped. "I can't believe my eyes. Oh, Mother, if you could see the beautiful dress she's wearing. And a hat with a feather. Why I hardly knew her!"

"And look what the blessed child has brought," Grannie said, holding out her apron where Heidi was piling roll after roll.

"I must go to Grandfather," Heidi said, taking off her hat. "But I'll come back tomorrow."

"What are you doing?" Brigitta asked as she watched

Heidi put on her battered straw hat.

"Grandfather won't know me if I wear that hat with the feather," Heidi said on her way out the door.

"Oh, he'll know you all right. Be careful, Heidi, he's very cross these days."

But Heidi was already running up the footpath. Several times she paused to catch her breath and to gaze at the mountain peaks blazing red in the setting sun. By the time she reached the hut, she was panting so hard that she just dropped her basket and fell into Grandfather's arms.

For a long time they sat quietly holding each other tightly. Grandfather had to swallow a lump in his throat before he could murmur, "So you've come home. Did they send you away?"

"Oh, no, Grandfather. They were very kind — Klara and Grandmamma and Herr Sesemann. But I was so homesick. I expect Herr Sesemann will tell you all about it in his letter." She jumped off Grandfather's lap and felt in her basket for the letter and the package.

After Grandfather had read the letter, he put the package on the bench between them. "This is yours," he explained. "Enough money to buy you a bed and clothes for many years."

"But I don't need money. Klara gave me more clothes than I'll ever need. And I already have a bed."

"Put the money away safely all the same. You'll find a use for it one day. Would you like a drink of milk?"

"Oh, yes! How I longed for Schwänli's milk when I was away."

Heidi was sitting in her old place at the table, hungrily drinking her second bowl of milk, when an earsplitting whistle sounded from up the mountain. She ran out just as Peter and the goats came racing down the slope.

"So you're back," Peter said, once he'd gotten over his astonishment. He could think of nothing more to say except, "Coming up the mountain with me tomorrow?"

"Not tomorrow," Heidi said, on her knees with her arms around Schwänli and Bärli. "I promised to visit your grandmother tomorrow. But I'll come soon."

Heidi led the two little goats off to their stalls, then returned to the hut to find Grandfather tucking her sheet around a new bed of fresh hay.

"How good it smells!" Heidi yawned. In no time she was asleep. She didn't stir even when Grandfather climbed the ladder to watch the moonlight shining on her face.

The next day Heidi and Grandfather set off down the mountain. At Peter's hut Heidi stopped for a visit while Grandfather went on to Dörfli to fetch her luggage.

"Ah, child," Grannie cried, "the roll was so tasty, so soft. I feel stronger already for eating one."

"But you must eat more than one, Grannie."

"Mother wants to make them last as long as possible," Brigitta explained.

"But they'll go stale!" Then Heidi remembered the package she'd carried home from Frankfurt. "I have lots of money," she said. "Peter shall take some to the village and fetch you a fresh roll every day."

"Oh no, child, we cannot —" Brigitta began.

"Yes," Heidi insisted. "A fresh roll every day and two on Sunday." Then she spotted the old book sitting on the shelf. "Shall I read to you, Grannie?"

Both women gasped. "Can you really read?"

Heidi climbed on a chair and brought down the hymnbook. "What would you like to hear?"

"Anything you like, child," said Grannie, her voice eager with expectation.

Heidi turned the pages, reading a line here and a line there. Soon she came to lines that seemed particularly special. "The Lord is my Shepherd," she read. "He maketh me to lie down in green pastures . . ."

By the time she had finished, Grannie's cheeks were wet with tears. "Dear child, what a blessing you are."

Later that evening, as Heidi and Grandfather sat out on the bench watching the setting sun, Heidi said, "Klara's Grandmamma was right. God had a reason for not letting me come home sooner."

Grandfather raised his eyebrows in surprise and Heidi

went on, "If I had come home when I first asked Him, I wouldn't have learned how to read. Now I can read Grannie's book to her. God arranged everything just as Grandmamma said He would. So now we'll pray to Him every night, won't we, Grandfather, so He will never forget us?"

Grandfather puffed on his pipe and stared off down the valley. "But," he said, almost to himself, "surely once a man has forgotten God and God has forgotten him, it is too late to go back."

"Oh, no, Grandfather! Grandmamma says one can always go back to God. A story in my book explains it all."

Heidi ran into the hut. The precious book was packed at the bottom of the basket she had carried up the mountain. In a moment Heidi was showing Grandfather the picture of a young man tending his father's flocks.

"But one day," she read, "he asked for half of his father's fortune, that he might go away and be his own master. He had no sooner reached the city than he gambled the money away. Hungry and cold, he went looking for work. The only work he could find was tending the swine . . ."

As Heidi read on through the Bible story of the Prodigal Son, Grandfather's eyes filled with tears.

"One day the young man was so sad and homesick that he decided to ask for his father's forgiveness. 'I am not worthy to be called your son,' he said when his father came running to meet him, 'but may I be one of your servants?' And what do you think, Grandfather? His father was not angry with him at all. Look at this picture. His father kisses him and takes him into the house and feeds him. Isn't that a wonderful story?"

Grandfather had to swallow several times before he could reply, "Yes, Heidi, a beautiful story."

The next morning, as church bells pealed from the valley below, Grandfather called up to the loft, "Come, Heidi, the sun is up. Put on your Sunday dress."

Heidi was amazed. "Are we going to church?" she asked, clambering down the ladder. "How fine you look, Grandfather! Silver buttons on your jacket. I've never seen you dressed that way before."

Grandfather just smiled and took her hand. As they walked down into the valley, the bells rang louder and louder, echoing among the mountains. In Dörfli the villagers were singing the first hymn when Heidi and her grandfather sat down at the back of the church. People began to whisper and look over their shoulders, but when the pastor started his sermon, all attention turned to him. He spoke so simply and warmly about forgiveness and love that after the service, people came up to shake Grandfather's hand as though he had always been one of them.

"What did I tell you?" said the carter who had carried Heidi and her trunk to Dörfli. "The child has changed him."

11

True to her promise, Klara wrote faithfully to Heidi, mentioning in every letter the promised trip to the mountains. But how can I wait a whole year to see her again? Heidi wondered.

To her surprise, the year passed quickly. After a summer on the Alps tending the goats, Heidi and Grandfather moved down to Dörfli, where they rented a little house. Heidi went to school every day and soon noticed what a poor student Peter was.

"You are going to learn to read," she said firmly, and despite his grumblings, she soon had him reciting his ABCs. By the end of the winter, he could even read some of the simpler hymns to Grannie.

Spring came at last. Mountain brooks, fed by melting snow, rushed down the slopes. Blue gentians and yellow buttercups dotted the new grass on the Alps. And Heidi, Grandfather, and the goats moved back to the hut.

One day, Peter arrived with the letter Heidi had been hoping for.

"Everything is packed for the journey," Klara wrote. "I can hardly wait to see you."

As Heidi read the letter out loud, Peter scowled. He didn't want interlopers spoiling his days with Heidi. Slashing about him with his stick, he drove the frightened goats up the mountain.

The day Klara was expected, Heidi sat out on Grandfather's bench watching for the visitors. Soon she saw an odd procession winding its way up the mountain. First came two men carrying Klara in a sedan chair, then a man with Klara's wheelchair upended on his head, then two with great baskets strapped to their backs. Finally came a man leading a white pony on which sat Grandmamma.

"My dear Alp Uncle," Grandmamma called as though she had known him all her life, "what a splendid view you have here!"

Grandfather lifted Klara gently from her sedan chair into her wheelchair. Heidi came running with blankets to tuck around her and at last the two girls were able to hug each other.

While Heidi pushed Klara in her chair so that she could see the goat shed and the singing fir trees and the

flower-strewn meadow, Grandfather brought out the table and chairs. Soon they were sitting down to a dinner of bread and tasty goat's cheese.

"Klara," Grandmamma exclaimed halfway through the meal, noticing her granddaughter reaching for more cheese. "Two helpings?"

"Everything tastes so much better here than in Frankfurt. I don't think I've ever been so hungry. Oh, Grandmamma, Heidi's been telling me all about the goats. How I wish I could see them! But we'll be gone before they come down from the high pasture."

Grandfather turned to Frau Sesemann. "If you would entrust Klara to our care and allow her to stay here for the summer, her health might benefit from our mountain air."

Heidi could hardly believe her ears. Eagerly, both girls looked at Frau Sesemann.

"My dear Uncle," she said, a twinkle in her eye, "you have read my mind."

When the hired men came toiling up the mountain again with the sedan chair and the white pony, only Frau Sesemann returned with them.

Of all the wonders of that wonderful day, the best for Klara came when she snuggled into the bed Grandfather made for her in the loft and looked through the round window at the starry sky.

"Oh, Heidi," she breathed, "being up here is like riding through the heavens."

The weeks passed happily for the two girls. Every morning Grandfather carried Klara down the ladder to her wheelchair. Heidi pushed her along the rocky path so they could collect flowers. Sometimes they just sat and talked or wrote letters to Grandmamma. Every morning and every evening Peter came by with the goats. Klara soon learned their names and longed to play with them, but Peter always brandished his stick and drove the goats past the hut as quickly as he could.

"That Peter," Heidi said crossly. "Sometimes I just don't understand him."

"Perhaps he's unhappy because you don't go up to the

alp with him," Klara said. "How I wish we could. How I would love to see the high meadow."

Klara was now drinking two bowls of goat's milk at each meal, just as Heidi did. Noticing this, Grandfather often went up the mountain and gathered tasty herbs to feed to Schwänli so that her milk would be even richer. Then one morning, as the girls were sitting under the fir trees, he said to Klara, "You look so much stronger, my child. Will you try, just once, to stand on the ground?"

Klara looked frightened. "It will hurt," she said.

"I'll hold you. Try just for a moment."

Because she wanted to please him, Klara gritted her teeth and tried. Clutching Grandfather's arm, she pulled herself up from the chair and stood on trembling legs.

"Wonderful!" Grandfather said, letting her down gently. Every day after that he coaxed her onto her feet again. Before long she had taken one shaky step and then another.

"Klara is so much stronger," Heidi said to Grandfather one day. "Do you think she might go up to the high pasture to spend a day with the goats?"

Grandfather stroked his beard for a few minutes. "We'll try it," he said finally.

The next morning at dawn Grandfather wheeled Klara's chair out of the shed where it was kept, then went to wake up the girls. As they were getting ready, Peter came along with the goats. He looked at the chair standing ready for the little invalid and suddenly the anger that had been bubbling up in him all summer boiled over. He grabbed the chair and gave it a mighty push. It crashed down the rocky slope and disappeared from sight. Only then did Peter realize what he'd done. Forgetting all about Schwänli and Bärli, he swung his stick and sent his goats charging up the mountain.

"Where is the chair?" Heidi asked when Grandfather carried Klara outside. She looked all around the hut. "Could the wind have blown it down the slope?"

"And where's Peter?" asked Grandfather. "Our goats are still in the shed."

"What shall I do without my chair?" Klara cried. "I shall never get to see the high alp."

"I'll carry you up," Grandfather said. "Then we'll see what happens."

When they reached the high meadow, they found the herd grazing peacefully, but Peter was nowhere to be seen.

After a few minutes, Heidi spotted him crouching behind a high rock.

"What's wrong with him, Grandfather?" she asked. "He acts just like a goat who expects a beating."

"Perhaps," Grandfather remarked dryly, as he settled Klara among her rugs and blankets, "perhaps he knows he deserves a beating."

After Grandfather left, Heidi brought Klara the tiniest of the goats to play with, then skipped off to pick a bouquet for her.

"If only you could see the bluebells nodding in the sunlight, Klara," Heidi said, returning with an armful of flowers. "I can almost hear their bells ringing." Heidi sat and looked at her friend for a moment, then suggested, "It's only a few steps up the mountain, around those rocks. If I held you, perhaps you could walk that far."

"Oh, no! You're much too small to hold me up."

"I'll ask Peter to help." Heidi ran up the mountain to where Peter lay staring sulkily into the distance.

"No!" he said, refusing to look at her.

Suddenly fed up with Peter's bad moods, Heidi stamped her foot and shouted, "You'd better come and help or you'll be sorry!"

Peter looked up in alarm. Did she know about the wheelchair? Would she tell the Alp Uncle? Although Heidi had only meant that she wouldn't give him the extra cheese and bread from their noon meal, Peter's guilty conscience made him get up instantly and follow her.

Between the two of them, they soon had Klara on her feet and struggling up the slope. It hurt more than Klara would let on. She had tears in her eyes and was breathing heavily by the time they reached the meadow full of bluebells.

"Oh, how beautiful!" she cried. "How glad I am that I could come here."

But Heidi was thinking how glad she was that they didn't have the wheelchair. Maybe without it Klara would try harder and harder to walk.

That evening, Heidi had a long, quiet talk with Grandfather and from then on, they both coaxed Klara to walk. As the days passed, her trembling steps grew more and more sure. When a letter arrived to say that Grandmamma and Herr Sesemann would be coming soon, the two girls decided to keep Klara's wonderful news a surprise.

The morning the visitors were expected, Heidi and Klara sat out on Grandfather's bench looking down over

the valley. At last Grandmamma, on a white pony, with Herr Sesemann walking beside her, came into view. When Grandmamma was close enough, she called out, "Klara, your chair, why aren't you in your chair?"

That was the signal the excited girls had been waiting for. Linking arms, they rose from the bench and began walking slowly forward. Even though Klara had to lean on Heidi, she was walking steadily on her own two feet.

"Look at me!" she cried, although her father and grandmother were already staring in open-mouthed amazement. "I can walk."

"My dear child, my dearest Klara!" They began to cry and laugh at the same time.

"A miracle, my dear Alp Uncle," Grandmamma said, when they were all sitting down around the table. "This is due to your help . . ."

"And the good mountain air," Grandfather said, beaming.

"And dear Schwänli's milk," added Klara.

Just then Peter's whistle sounded and he and the goats came bounding down the mountain. Grandmamma and Herr Sesemann were enchanted to see the animals they had heard so much about.

"Come here, my boy," Grandmamma called.

Stricken with terror at the sight of the grand lady from Frankfurt, Peter began babbling the minute he was close to her, "I'm sorry! I didn't mean to. And now it's all broken in pieces."

Grandmamma turned puzzled eyes on the Alp Uncle. "What is wrong with the boy?"

"I imagine," Grandfather said, frowning so that Peter trembled even more, "he is feeling guilty. Peter is the wind that blew the wheelchair down the mountain. And now he fears he will be punished."

Grandmamma looked back at Peter's terrified face

and said, "No, my dear Uncle. The boy has been punished enough already. But here is something to think about, Peter." She reached out and took the goatherd's hands so that he had to look directly into her eyes. "Anyone who does a wrong deed and thinks no one will know is mistaken. God always knows. This time He turned wickedness into good, for Klara tried even harder to walk once she lost her chair. But you must remember always to think before you are tempted to do a wicked act. Do you understand?"

Peter nodded.

Grandmamma smiled and patted his hand. "Now I would like to give you a present to remember the people from Frankfurt. What would you like most in the world?"

Peter could hardly believe his ears. A present? Anything in the world? And then he asked for something he had never had. "A penny," he said quickly. "To spend at the fair in Mayenfeld."

Grandmamma smiled and took a dollar from her purse. "Here we have a hundred pennies," she said, and then she added four more pennies. "Now you have two for every week of the year." Then she called Heidi over. "And you, dear child, what present would you like?"

Heidi didn't need to think. She knew exactly what she wanted. "The bed I had in Frankfurt," she said. "For Peter's grannie, so she'll never have to sleep in a cold, hard bed again."

"Dear child," Grandmamma said, kissing her, "it shall be sent the minute we are back home."

Klara spent one last night in the loft bedroom under the stars. The next morning, when it was time for Grandfather to carry her down the mountain to the waiting carriage, both girls were in tears.

"Summer will come again," Heidi promised, trying to smile. "And just think, Klara, next year you'll be much stronger. We'll run up to the high alp together and lie in the field of bluebells and play with the goats. Life will be wonderful!"

And so it was.